WINTER WITHOUT SALT

BY *Georgiana Dorcas Ceder*

Illustrated by CHARLES WALKER

WILLIAM MORROW & COMPANY, *New York, 1962*

Library of Congress Catalog Card Number 62-7128

CONTENTS

WINTER WITHOUT SALT

CHAPTER 1

A Doe and a Buck

THE February wind, gusty and cold, tugged at the bare branches on the wooded Kentucky hillside. It pressed Peter Rowan's buckskins tight against him. It whipped the tail of his coonskin cap against his face, as he plodded along after Uncle Jim.

With a quick jerk of his head Peter tossed the tail over his shoulder. "Wish we were heading home," he said to Uncle Jim. "Aunt Libby would have the fire roaring." He glanced up. "Sky's darkening. Reckon it's getting late."

"I'd like to get more than this," said Uncle Jim. He nodded toward the pole they carried between them. A furry raccoon, a possum, and an empty trap hung from it.

Pausing to stir some brown oak leaves with his foot, he remarked, "That trap we set was hereabouts." Uncovering it, he grunted, "Hump!"

Peter bent down for a closer look. "Sprung!" he exclaimed. "But nothing's caught."

"A few brown hairs," said Uncle Jim. "Mink, most likely." He picked up the trap and hung it on the pole. "We'll go down a ways toward the trail. Might get something there."

They walked on, but suddenly Uncle Jim stopped and motioned to Peter to lower the pole they carried. A little way ahead, beyond a patch of hazel shrub, Peter saw a doe. Uncle Jim crept within range, aimed, and fired. The doe fell.

Peter went on alone until a rustling sound nearby, among some scrub oaks, made him glance that way. A buck was standing there. He'll take off, if I call Uncle Jim. I'd best try for him, Peter decided quickly. His hands trembled as he aimed and fired. Holding his breath, he watched the buck leap high, jump again, run a little way, stumble and fall!

"What'd you get?" Uncle Jim called out, hurrying back toward Peter.

"Buck," he answered, pointing. "There!"

"Good shot!" exclaimed Uncle Jim.

Peter's heart was thumping. He took a few steps toward the buck, but Uncle Jim caught his shoulder and held him fast. "Always reload first," he warned. "Can't tell what you'll meet up with next."

Peter's blue eyes shone with excitement, but his hands steadied as he cleaned his gun and Uncle Jim took care of his. Peter poured in some powder from their powder horn, put in a bit of cloth, rammed it down, and slipped in a ball. Then, gun loaded, he hurried toward the fallen buck.

Its sides heaved once and its legs twitched as Peter came near. He stopped and watched. It was hard to believe he had shot it. They'd sure have plenty of meat for a while. When the buck lay still, Peter came close and put his hand on the spreading antlers.

"He's a big fellow," said Uncle Jim, coming after him. "Make a fine buckskin when the hide's dressed."

"Could I do it?" Peter asked eagerly. "By myself?"

"Think you could?" asked Uncle Jim, rubbing his chin. "Takes a lot of rubbing."

"I could do it real good," urged Peter. "I've helped rub salt."

"I know," said Uncle Jim with a nod. Then he added, "We have to be careful of salt. Have to fetch it a long way." He walked around looking at nearby trees. "Reckon we can't take him along with us. The doe's all we can tote."

Peter caught his breath. Leave the buck, his buck, way off here? All night? He swallowed hard.

"That buck weighs near a hundred and fifty pounds," said Uncle Jim. "We'll hang him yonder, in that tree. We can ride Lady back here tomorrow, make a sledge, and haul him home."

Peter could see that was the best way, but he put his hand on the antlers and looked questioningly at his uncle.

Uncle Jim had a twinkle in his eyes. "We'll cut those off," he said, "and fetch them along with us."

Together they dragged the buck to the tree, hoisted it up, and settled it firmly in the crotch. Then, sniffing the air, Uncle Jim said, "We'd best turn back. It's fixing to storm. Sleet, maybe, or snow."

They added the doe and the antlers to the game on the pole. Uncle Jim helped to raise one end of it to Peter's shoulder; then he took the other end himself, and they started for home.

When they stopped to rest, Uncle Jim remarked, "It's just a couple of years now since you started hunting. You're doing right well."

Peter looked down at the gun in his hand. He remembered when Uncle Jim had given it to him, year before last, when he was past ten.

"Reckon it's time you learned to use this," Uncle Jim had said, "so you can help take care of our folks."

That meant Mary Ann, Peter's sister, a year older than he, Cousin David, just past five, and Aunt Libby, who'd been looking after Mary Ann and Peter since their mother had died, back in Stanford.

As they walked on again, Uncle Jim said, "You're taking after your pappy. Reckon you could pretty near hit anything you was aiming for."

Peter nodded. Maybe even a redskin, he added to himself, and gripped his gun more firmly. If they came round, he'd shoot fast. Never know when Indians are coming, he thought. I wonder if any of them could be hereabouts now. What if they were and found his buck? "Think it's safe, the buck?" he asked anxiously. "From redskins, I mean?"

"Seen any signs?" asked Uncle Jim gravely.

"No," murmured Peter. He listened hard. There was only the sound of the wind in the trees and a soft swishing as their moccasins brushed fallen leaves.

The pole they were carrying seemed to grow heavier and heavier. It was an uphill walk to the cabin, and they stopped to rest several times. It was growing dark when they reached a rail fence. A barn, a pigpen, and a little smokehouse made shadows at the far side of the clearing. In the center of the open space stood a cabin, close to an old spreading beech tree. Sparks drifted upward from the wide stone chimney. The wind caught them and carried them high.

Uncle Jim slid the bars of the rail fence to one side.

"Nip's barking loud," said Peter with a grin. "Reckon he hears us coming."

The cabin door swung open wide. A black-and-white hound dog bounded out, yelping and barking a welcome. After him trotted small, tow-headed David, crying, "What'd you get, Pappy?"

"You're letting out all the heat," Aunt Libby called after him. She closed the door part way. A moment later, with a scarf over her head, she followed him.

Mary Ann came too. The wind loosened wisps of dark curls around her face. She put up her hands to hold them in place, and said as she came near, "You got possum, and coon, and deer?"

"I see antlers!" exclaimed Aunt Libby.

Peter stretched himself as tall as he could and said proudly, "I got a buck, too." He carried the guns into the cabin and placed them on pegs behind the door. Near them he hung the powder horn and shot bag.

Uncle Jim told the family about the buck. "It was a good shot for a twelve-year-old," he said.

"Peter's like his pappy," said Aunt Libby, and smiled at him as he came out. "Supper's near ready. The pigs are in the pen, and I've fed Lady and milked Belle." She lifted her long linsey-woolsey skirt and stepped lightly to the cabin.

"I'll take in the antlers," said Mary Ann.

Peter handed them to her. Turning, he gave David a happy poke in the ribs, and whispered, "I shot a buck, a big, big buck!" Then he grasped one end of the pole to help carry the game to the smokehouse.

"I'll stop at the barn," said Uncle Jim. "Make sure everything's right."

"I'm going with you," said David.

Bits of ice stung Peter's face on his way back to the cabin. My buck will be coated with ice by morning, he thought, but ice won't hurt it any. He picked up the traps, dropped them near the cabin door, and stepped inside.

CHAPTER 2

A Sound in the Night

Aunt Libby lifted the cover of the bake pot, sitting on the glowing embers of the fire, and took out the steaming corn bread. "Is that stew sticking to the pot?" she asked Mary Ann.

"I'll see," answered Mary Ann, and swung the black kettle, hanging from the crane, away from the fire.

Peter watched as she stirred the stew. Her face was rosy from the heat, two neat dark braids hung down her back.

"Squirrel stew will taste just right," he said, and

19

turned to hang up his coonskin cap and deerskin jacket. He unfastened his moccasins, slipped them off, and wiggled his cold toes in the bearskin that covered part of the rough puncheon floor. The furry warmth felt good. It was good to be home, good, too, to think about shooting the buck.

"Wash up," Aunt Libby told him. "The bucket's by the door. We brought it in so the water wouldn't freeze. It'll be right cold tonight. Will you fetch him a towel, Mary Ann?"

"See you hang it up," ordered Mary Ann, in a big sister tone. She handed it to him, then dodged out of reach when Peter tried to catch one of her braids.

He scrubbed his face and hands until they tingled, while Mary Ann put things on the table—wooden bowls for stew, gourds for milk, horn spoons and forks carved from cane.

When David and Nip and Uncle Jim came in, Aunt Libby said, "Set to the table. I'm dishing up the stew."

After they had eaten Aunt Libby's spinning wheel was moved near the firelight. Humming a tune, she made the wheel turn. Uncle Jim added a big log to the fire, then brought out a dish of bear grease. "Reckon we'd best soften our moccasins," he said.

"They'll be stiff and hard, come morning, if you don't," remarked Aunt Libby. She smiled as Peter fetched his moccasins and began to rub grease well into the skin.

Mary Ann and David settled themselves on the hearth, cracking walnuts and taking out the meats. Nip snuggled close to David and went to sleep. As he threw some nutshells into the fire David said, "What'll you do with the buck, Peter?"

Before he could answer Aunt Libby said, with a laugh, "We'll have roast venison, and your pappy will trade the skin for wool, so I can make linsey-woolsey shirts for you all, and maybe a dress for Mary Ann."

"A red one maybe," murmured Mary Ann dreamily, resting her head against Aunt Libby's knee.

"We could hang up the antlers," suggested Peter, glancing around the cabin. Reckon they could hang over that shelf where my father's fiddle is, he thought. Closing his eyes, he knew just how they'd look there. Slowly and more slowly, he rubbed grease on his moccasins.

"Peter!" Aunt Libby was shaking his shoulder. "Get up to bed. You're asleep sitting up."

"David should be in bed too," said Mary Ann. She led him to the small room at the other end of the cabin.

Peter climbed the ladder to the loft. Little flickerings of light shone through the cracks in the floor from the room below. He felt his way to the place where the chimney went through to the roof. On one side of it, where it was warmest and driest, were two large dried gourds for storing salt. On the other side was Peter's cornhusk bed. The husks rustled softly when he lay down and pulled the bearskin cover up to his ears.

The wind roared down the chimney and whistled round the cabin. Sleet tapped lightly against the logs and the roof. Peter ducked his head well under the cover. He thought about the antlers again before he fell asleep. He'd keep them always. Besides them, he had his father's gun and fiddle. Someday, maybe, he'd get strings for it and learn to play when Aunt Libby sang. . . .

In the night he wakened and sat up, listening. What was it, that sound? It came again. A horse? Stumbling? From the room below he heard a low warning growl. Nip growling?

For a moment he lay still. Then he slid from beneath the warm cover and, shivering, climbed down the ladder. Uncle Jim was dressed and stood near the door, listening.

"Heard something," whispered Peter.

Uncle Jim nodded. "So did Nip."

Aunt Libby tied on her apron and straightened the bed covers. She murmured softly, "Could be an animal prowling." Her voice trembled, "Or a . . ." She didn't say it, but Peter knew she was thinking an Indian.

He felt goose-pimply all over. Pressing one fist hard against his other hand, he tried to stop the shivers. "It was like a horse, stumbling, or shying a stone," he whispered. "Should I go to the barn?"

"No!" Aunt Libby put her arm around him. "Wait."

Uncle Jim rubbed his chin thoughtfully. "We'll see, when it's light." In a lower tone he added, "Redskins don't usually come round this time of year."

He lifted the guns from the pegs back of the door, looked them over carefully, and placed them on the table. "If they're coming, we'll be ready," he said grimly. Then he added to Aunt Libby, "Wake the young'uns. Best get them dressed."

She stepped quickly into their little room. Peter heard her whispering to Mary Ann and rousing David.

"They'll be signaling, if they're hereabouts," said Uncle Jim. "Daybreak's the time they would attack."

Peter bent his head listening for the hoot of an owl or, perhaps, the short, sharp bark of a fox that wasn't a fox. A tightness grew inside of him. "It would be a sight easier to do something," he whispered, "instead of just sitting."

A moment later he suggested, "Might be I'd see something from the loft."

Uncle Jim nodded and Peter climbed up. He crawled over a pile of skins to a small shuttered opening, unfastened the latch, and slowly, quietly lifted the shutter to look out.

The wind had died. A break in the clouds and a streak of light showed in the east. Ice on the branches began to glisten as the sky brightened. With keen eyes Peter searched for shadows or a movement among the trees or along the fence. "It's sure light enough now," he told himself. "Redskins would be yelling all over the place, if they were around." Carefully he closed and fastened the shutter.

"Nothing to see," he said, coming down the ladder.

Uncle Jim unlatched the door. "Keep watch. I'm going to the barn."

Peter took a gun from the table. Aunt Libby picked up another one. She murmured, as she came to stand close beside Peter at the door, "I can shoot too."

She's afraid, thought Peter. He edged closer to her. I'll look out for her, same as if she was my own mother.

Uncle Jim's footsteps crunched on the frosty ground. He walked to the barn, went in, and soon came out. When he was back in the cabin, he said, "Everything's just as it was last night."

Gun across his lap, Peter sat down. Nip came and nosed his knee. "Good dog," he said, pulling Nip's ears. "We sure heard something . . . mighty like a horse."

Uncle Jim drew his brows together in a puzzled frown. "We're too far from the trail to hear a horse going past on it. We'd best look around some more. I'll step up to the big rock, overlooking the valley, and see what there's to see."

Still holding his gun, Peter followed Uncle Jim out of the cabin and watched him disappear into

the woods. "I'll look around some too," he decided
suddenly.

"Where are you going?" asked Aunt Libby.

"Over toward the cornfield," he answered.

"Don't go far, Peter," she called after him softly.
"Be careful. . . ."

"If there's redskins around, I'll get one afore
they find our cabin, or get me," he promised himself grimly.

Quickly he crossed the clearing and slid between the rails of the fence, near the pigpen.
There were pig tracks everywhere in the frozen
ground. Indians might have seen and followed
them. He ran to a pine tree, pressed himself between its heavy branches, and listened. There was
no sound but the pounding of his own heart.

From one tree to another he moved cautiously,
watching for Indian signs—footprints or broken
twigs. He was near the corn patch when he stood
still. "Sure's I'm alive and breathing," he whispered, "a horse is neighing yonder off to the left."

Peter turned and walked in that direction.

CHAPTER 3

A Stranger

AFTER walking a little way and hearing nothing more, Peter stopped and looked around. Suddenly, close by, a branch cracked sharply. He flattened himself against a tree and waited, hardly breathing. It could be a coon or a turkey, he thought, or the ice breaking a branch. Then someone began to talk, in a deep, rumbling voice, not at all like Uncle Jim's.

Chills raced up Peter's back. Redskins? In that hollow, just past those bushes? I'd best find Uncle

Jim, quick. But first I ought to see how many of them there are.

Creeping to the bushes, he peered between the branches. There was a big dappled gray horse tied to a tree. Beyond the horse, a stranger knelt on the ground.

Peter took a long breath. "He's not a redskin," he said to himself, "nor a settler either, wearing that long black cloak. Who all is he talking with that I can't see?" He leaned to one side, then to the other, and drew his brows together in a frown. Then he edged nearer to listen to what the man was saying.

"Thank Thee, Lord, for the daylight, and for keeping me through the stormy night."

"He's praying!" whispered Peter with surprise. "Like that preacher man that came to Stanford." Will he stop at the cabin? he wondered eagerly. Aunt Libby would be liking that, and Uncle Jim, too.

The young man got up and put on his wide-brimmed hat. He brushed some leaves and bits of ice from his knees and cloak, and went to his horse. "We're cold, Silver Boy, and hungry," he said, stroking the animal, "but the Lord will help us."

The horse answered with a soft whinny. The man untied the reins, drew them over the horse's head, and put one foot in a stirrup.

Peter got to his feet quickly and called out, as he came from behind the bushes, "Howdy."

At the sound of his voice the horse reared. With a bound the man lifted himself into the saddle. He sat easily and firmly, quieting the horse.

Peter's eyes shone as he watched. When the horse, breathing hard, stood still, Peter spoke again. "I wasn't aiming to scare him. You sure can handle him good."

"Good morning," said the man smiling warmly. "We're glad to see you. We've been stumbling over this hill most of the night."

Peter nodded. "We were afeared it was redskins."

"God forbid!" exclaimed the man. "By His grace I escaped them. Tell me, are there settlers near here?"

"Just my folks," answered Peter. "They'd sure be proud to have you stop by."

"Thank you," said the man. "Indeed, I'll be glad to."

"Ain't been anyone come this way since we've

been here," said Peter, turning and leading the way.

The man, riding the big horse, followed. "When did you come?" he asked.

"Three years ago, come summer," answered Peter. "Afore that we stayed in Stanford while Uncle Jim was clearing some land and building the cabin."

They hadn't gone far when they saw Uncle Jim striding toward them. "Morning," he called out. "Saw a trail, up by the big rock. Followed it downhill."

"That rock sheltered me last night," said the stranger with a smile. "I'm Daniel Clark. Most folks call me Mr. Dan. I travel these backwoods trails to bring the Church to settlements where there is no church."

"Circuit rider?" said Uncle Jim. Coming near, he held out his hand. "Jim Rowan's my name. This here's my nephew, Peter." The two men shook hands.

"Yesterday afternoon," Mr. Dan said, "I ran into a party of Indians. There were more than a dozen of them, and they seemed to have extra horses."

"Horse raiders, most likely," said Uncle Jim. His tone was grim.

"How'd you get away," asked Peter.

"I made off, as fast as I could in the opposite direction," Mr. Dan answered. "I hoped they hadn't seen me. I thought with the noise of their horses they wouldn't notice mine. They seemed in a great hurry, going north."

"Aiming to get across the river," said Uncle Jim quietly.

Mr. Dan continued. "An hour or so later, when I stopped to let my horse drink, I heard horses coming back of me. Fearing I had been followed, I led Silver Boy away from the trail, along the water and up a rocky bank. Then I waited and watched from behind some rocks. Two Indians came along, riding fast."

"Raiders?" asked Uncle Jim.

Mr. Dan hesitated. "Perhaps," he said. "I decided to let them get well ahead of me and waited. I was just ready to lead Silver Boy back to the trail and start on, when two Indians came riding back."

"Same ones?" asked Uncle Jim shortly.

"I believe so," answered Mr. Dan. "It had started to sleet and I couldn't see clearly. I thought they were seeking my trail, but they went on." He paused and added, "Between them, I think, they carried something on a pole. When I could no longer hear them, I started out. By that time it was dark, and I lost my way in the storm."

Uncle Jim spoke slowly. "Seems likely they were raiders. When they lost your track, they turned back. After horses, they were."

Settlers' horses, thought Peter, settlers, like us. He asked anxiously, "Those settlers will get their horses back, won't they?"

"Reckon not," answered Uncle Jim. "Afore they can get together and start after them, redskins and horses will be over the river, in Indian territory."

In sober silence they walked on until Peter exclaimed, "If settlers can't get them back, soldiers should do it. Go after those redskins and kill them all!"

"Killing doesn't help." Mr. Dan spoke quickly. He added, "Not all Indians are bad . . . not all white men are good."

Peter kicked a pebble out of the path. How could anyone say that? He opened the bars of the fence and glanced up at the man on the horse as he rode into the clearing. Reckon a circuit rider wouldn't know much about redskins, Peter decided.

"Peter will look after your horse," said Uncle Jim.

"I'll take my saddlebags," said Mr. Dan. "Perhaps news from the outside world and the word of God will help to repay your kindness." He dismounted, unfastened the straps, and lifted the bulging bags from the back of his horse. Then, handing the reins to Peter, he looked straight at him and smiled, his eyes crinkling up at the corners.

Peter smiled back. Mr. Dan's my friend, he thought. I found him. He liked the way the circuit rider talked and the way he looked when he smiled. And he sure could get on and off a horse in a hurry.

When Peter led Silver Boy into the barn, Lady put her head over the partition. She rolled her eyes, flattened her ears, and watched when Peter brought water and cane for the other horse.

"Want some, too?" Peter stepped over to Lady and stroked her soft nose. "If those redskins had come this way, we'd have gone after them, for sure."

Silver Boy neighed and shivered. "Reckon you're needing a rubdown," said Peter, going back to him. As he stood beside the big horse, rubbing his flanks, he thought of the way the circuit rider had mounted. "Wonder, could I get up like that?"

he asked himself. He stood on the lower bar of the stall, getting ready to jump, when Uncle Jim came.

Peter stepped down quickly. "What's he doing?" he asked.

"Resting," answered Uncle Jim. "He's chilled to the bone."

"His horse was hungry," said Peter. He added, "So am I."

"Fire's going," said Uncle Jim. "We'll eat soon." He brought a pail and a low stool. "Milking time, Belle."

When Peter had finished rubbing down Silver Boy, he brought water and cane for Lady and Belle.

David, with Nip after him, came tearing across the clearing to the barn. "Mammy says," he shouted breathlessly, "bring a piggin of water and don't make noise. The man's sleeping."

Peter grinned. "Listen to him," he said. "And his mammy said 'don't make noise.'" He took a bucket, hurried to fill it at the spring, and carried it in.

There was a strange feeling of excitement in the cabin, though Mr. Dan was not in sight. Still sleeping in the loft, Peter decided.

Mary Ann tiptoed to the bucket to dip water

into the kettle. Her braids were wound round her head and pinned with some of Aunt Libby's skewers.

"Acting grown-up and important?" asked Peter, itching to give her braids a yank.

"Shush," whispered Mary Ann. "Mr. Dan's sleeping."

Aunt Libby was trying to hush David. "Yes," she said softly, "he'll stay the night. He's a circuit rider."

"What's that?" demanded David.

She explained quietly. "A man who goes from place to place."

"Why does he go?" persisted David.

"To tell folks about God," answered his mother. She put some ash cakes on the fire. "When a circuit rider comes, all the folks nearby have a meeting."

Mary Ann hung the full kettle on the crane over the fire. "I remember," she said. "Aunt Libby took us to some meetings when we were in Stanford. A man talked and prayed."

"The folks sang, too," added Peter.

Then Uncle Jim brought in the warm milk, and Aunt Libby said, "We'll be needing something for supper."

"Something special like, for company?" asked

Uncle Jim. His tone was teasing and his eyes were twinkling.

Aunt Libby tilted her head and Uncle Jim chuckled. "Peter got a turkey last week. It's hanging in the smokehouse."

CHAPTER 4

Going for the Buck

"WHEN are we going after the buck?" Peter asked
when breakfast was over.

"Aunt Libby's got a mind to roast a turkey while
we're gone," said Uncle Jim. "Reckon she'll need a
sight of wood."

Peter wished they could start right off. He
wanted to fetch the buck home, so they could all
see it—Mr. Dan, too. Why did Uncle Jim chop so
much wood? They could cut more when they got
back. He lugged in the chunks and helped David
to gather up the chips.

"Should I ready Lady?" he asked, and Uncle Jim nodded.

Peter harnessed the horse and led her out. He waited while Uncle Jim stacked the rest of the wood near the door. He tucked his ax into his belt and took Lady's reins, while Peter brought their guns, shot bag, and powder horn from the cabin.

"We're going, too," said David. "Me and Nip." He trotted back of Lady as Uncle Jim walked her to the fence.

"No," Uncle Jim told him. "You're staying here. And mind you look after Mammy and Mary Ann. Don't wander off."

"But I want to see the buck," pleaded David.

"We'll be back afore dark," said his father.

Peter opened the bars of the fence. When Lady had walked through the opening, Uncle Jim mounted. He reached down with his strong hand and gave Peter a lift up behind him.

Riding through the woods a warm excitement filled Peter. He wished Lady would get a move on her, but Uncle Jim let her take her own gait.

The sun sparkled and ice melted and dripped from the trees. "It's warming up," remarked Uncle Jim. "It'll be time soon for getting in the seed."

"Reckon so," murmured Peter. Time enough to

think about planting, after they had got the buck home. If Uncle Jim let him cure it, he'd sure do it good. They would have a buckskin to trade with their other skins. "When you aiming to go," he asked. "To trade, I mean."

"After planting," answered Uncle Jim.

Lady walked on. At last they reached the spot where they had shot the buck and the doe. Uncle Jim stopped Lady and got off her back. "These saplings will be just about right for making a sledge," he said. Taking his ax from his belt he began to chop at a slender tree.

"I'm going yonder to see the buck," said Peter and slid down from Lady's back.

Hurrying to the tree, where they had left the buck, he looked up, then glanced around, puzzled. "Uncle Jim!" he shouted. "Come, come quick!"

A few long strides and Uncle Jim stood beside him. He looked up and then down at the ground. "Gone!" he said quietly. "And it wasn't wildcats or wolves that did it. The bones would still be here."

Gone? Peter could hardly believe it. He felt empty and sick. "Who . . ." he began.

Uncle Jim interrupted. "Indians. Probably the same two that followed Mr. Dan. Reckon they found deer tracks crossing the trail and followed them till they came on the buck."

Anger flared hotly inside of Peter. "Thieving redskins!" he cried. "Nothing's safe from them." As they mounted, he added in a hard voice, "Sure wish I could get at them." He clutched his gun tightly.

"I've known the feeling," Uncle Jim told him. "But the circuit rider's got a point. Killing don't help none."

"It was my buck," said Peter. "I shot it, and I wanted to cure the skin myself."

"There'll be other bucks," Uncle Jim's voice was quiet. "You can help cure the doe."

Helping's not like doing it myself, Peter grumbled to himself as Lady jogged along. Uncle Jim ought to know that.

David and Nip were waiting for them at the fence. "Where is it, the big buck? Didn't you fetch it?" David's piping voice carried across the clearing. Aunt Libby and Mary Ann heard it and hurried out of the cabin. Mr. Dan came out of the barn.

"Where'd you leave the buck?" asked Aunt Libby.

Peter felt too choked to answer. It was hard

enough to lose a buck without having to talk about it.

Uncle Jim told them. "Judging by the signs, a couple of Indians made off with it."

"Those two last night!" exclaimed Mr. Dan. "I thought they were carrying something." He shook his head. "That's too bad."

"It was my brother's," cried Mary Ann. Her eyes flashed.

"Indians reckon everything here belongs to them," said Uncle Jim. He looked at each of them and added, "We don't like losing the buck. But we might have lost a sight more. If they'd come here, they might have set the place afire, or run off with Lady."

Aunt Libby nodded. Her lips were pressed tightly together and her face looked white.

"They didn't come though," Uncle Jim added quietly, "and I'm not expecting them. But we'll keep watch, even though we haven't seen any of them since we've been here."

"We saw enough trouble with them on our way to Stanford," murmured Aunt Libby. She turned to Mary Ann. "We'd best get back to our cooking."

As they returned to the cabin, Mr. Dan remarked, "I understand you settled here about three years ago."

Uncle Jim nodded. "Afore that the family stayed in Stanford a couple of years, while I readied this place. We came from Virginia about five years back. In ninety-three, it was, the year after Kentucky became the fifteenth state."

"You're off the beaten track," said Mr. Dan.

"Yes," agreed Uncle Jim. "But I get supplies and trade skins about twice a year." He led Lady into the barn, and Mr. Dan followed.

Peter got a piggin and went to the spring to fetch water for Lady. When he came into the barn, Mr. Dan and Uncle Jim were talking while Uncle Jim worked.

Mr. Dan talked about a paper printed in Lexington, and postriders who brought letters, and a road wide enough for wagons to come over. "The country is growing fast," he said. He told about settlements to the south and to the northwest, along the Ohio River.

Peter climbed to the loft and threw down some cornstalks. He carried them to the cabin, opened the door, and called out, "Brought stalks for a bed."

Aunt Libby poured sizzling pan drippings over

the roasting turkey. "Get up in the loft," she said. "Mary Ann can hand up a few stalks at a time. Mind you have plenty. Mr. Dan's a tall man."

When Peter came down, she said, "We're getting supper early, so we'll have a long evening for talk. Fetch in some wood."

He dragged in a couple of big logs. As he dumped them near the fireplace he saw the antlers in the corner. They're all I got from shooting a buck, he thought sadly. Redskins, most likely, are roasting and eating it this very night.

CHAPTER 5

The Circuit Rider Talks

Aunt Libby and Mary Ann went to the loft to fix a bed for the circuit rider. They were shoving things around up there when Mr. Dan and Uncle Jim came in and sat down at one side of the fireplace.

David climbed on his father's knee. Peter settled himself on the floor, his back against the log wall. He listened as the circuit rider and Uncle Jim talked.

"Your wife told me about your home in Virginia," said Mr. Dan. "What made you decide to leave it and come here?"

Uncle Jim thought a moment. "It was a chance to get new, good land, and more of it. We heard plenty of talk about Kentucky and the hunting, and my brother, Peter's father, had been here."

"Oh," said Mr. Dan. "Is your brother with you?"

"Killed," answered Uncle Jim. "Indians. On our way into Kentucky, up near Crab Orchard."

No one spoke for a while. Peter looked into the fire A blue flame crept like a shadow along the log. Suddenly it flared upward, red and yellow, like redskins jumping from behind some trees. A knot in the log cracked sharply, like the sound of a gun!

Peter started and looked up. Mr. Dan's eyes seemed sad. "Indian ways and our ways are different," he said. "White men have not always treated them fairly. Perhaps, if they had, things might be better." He sighed deeply. "It's the law of tooth and claw."

"A life for a life," added Uncle Jim, in a low voice.

That's right, thought Peter. Redskins killed settlers, like my pappy. Why shouldn't Indians be killed? They steal, too, horses and bucks. He set his jaw hard and frowned.

"There is another law," Mr. Dan was saying, "that you love one another."

That means our own folks, Peter told himself quickly, but not redskins. Mr. Dan couldn't mean that. Peter glanced at Uncle Jim, waiting for him to speak.

Uncle Jim looked grave, and said slowly, "That's hard sometimes."

"Yes," agreed Mr. Dan. "I know it is."

Aunt Libby and Mary Ann came down from the loft. "Set to the table," said Aunt Libby. She lifted the golden brown turkey onto a large wooden trencher.

When they were seated around the table, Mr. Dan said, "Let us give thanks for the fellowship of friends and for this food." Bowing his head, he closed his eyes, and they all prayed.

Then Uncle Jim carved the turkey, and Mr. Dan remarked, "I see you have a violin."

Uncle Jim nodded. "It was my brother's."

Aunt Libby spoke up. "Peter has a hankering to play it, but the strings are broken."

"My mammy sings," chirped David. "About the blackbird."

After supper Mr. Dan opened his saddlebags and took out a book and a paper. "Here's the

Gazette I mentioned, published in Lexington." He handed the paper to Uncle Jim.

"Thanks," said Uncle Jim. He held the paper toward the firelight to read. Peter looked over his shoulder.

"Do you read, Peter?" asked Mr. Dan.

"I learned the letters when we were in Stanford," answered Peter. "But I've most forgotten them by now." He sat down again on the floor and hugged his knees.

When Aunt Libby and Mary Ann sat down, Mr. Dan began to talk. "God speaks to us in this Book," he said. Opening it he read about loving God with all your heart.

Peter listened. Reckon most folks love God, he thought. Mr. Dan does for sure, because he's a preacher and it's in his Book. But is loving redskins in his Book, too?

When Mr. Dan paused and glanced up, Peter asked, "Does it say anything about Indians?"

Mr. Dan turned some pages and answered thoughtfully, "It bids us love our neighbors."

"Folks living close by," said Peter quickly.

"Not always," said Mr. Dan smiling. "You were helpful and kind to me today."

"Glad to have you here," said Uncle Jim heartily.

"But redskins aren't neighbors," said Peter.

"Let me tell you a story," said Mr. Dan. "A man was traveling on a dreary, lonely road, and robbers attacked him. They took everything he had, even his clothes."

"Redskins, most likely," said Peter.

Mr. Dan shook his head. "No, they were not Indians. Several travelers from the man's own country came along. They heard his cries for help, but they did not stop. At last a stranger came along. When he heard the cries of the wounded man, he stopped and knelt beside him. He brought him to an inn and paid the innkeeper to take care of him. That man, who helped, was a good neighbor," Mr. Dan said quietly.

"Was he an Indian?" asked Peter.

"No, neither man was," answered Mr. Dan. "The story tells us, though, who our neighbors are. They are folks who need our help and love. That means Indians, too."

He closed the Book and handed it to Aunt Libby. "You mentioned that you lost your Bible on the way to Kentucky. I'll leave this one with you. I have others in my saddlebags."

"Do you know the song," he asked, *"O God Our Help in Ages Past?"*

"My, yes!" exclaimed Aunt Libby. "It's an old song. We sang it lots of times, back in Virginia."

Mr. Dan began to sing.

> O God our help in ages past,
>   Our hope for years to come,
> Our shelter from the stormy blast,
>   And our eternal home. . . .

Aunt Libby and Uncle Jim joined in the singing. Mary Ann hummed along, not knowing the words. David had fallen asleep. He woke up and sat rubbing his eyes.

Peter listened, tapping out the rhythm of the tune with his fingers on the floor. If there were strings to the fiddle, he thought, I could be playing that tune for them.

The evening had gone fast. Peter led the way to the loft. Aunt Libby had made a bed for Mr. Dan close to the big gourds that held their salt.

"What wonderful smells there are up here," remarked Mr. Dan, as he lay down. "Dried mint, sassafras, and bay leaves."

Peter was used to the smells. He had helped to store things in the loft. There was a big bin filled with ears of corn to be shelled for seed. The dark pile at the other end of the loft was the furs they'd been collecting. Over his head pieces of pumpkins, strung on strings, hung from the rafters. Under the eaves there were pumpkins and turnips.

Mr. Dan fell asleep quickly. Peter listened to his deep breathing. As he lay awake, he thought over the story of the good neighbor. Be neighbors to redskins? Help them, love them? Under the covers he squirmed and clenched his fists. Indians killed my pappy, wounded my mammy, and broke her heart grieving for him. Yesterday they stole my buck. They're not neighbors to us, and I don't want to be neighbors to them.

CHAPTER 6

Salt and Skins

PETER hurried down from the loft the next morning looking for the circuit rider.

Aunt Libby smiled at him. "Mr. Dan was off afore daybreak," she said. Then she added, "No need to feel down. He'll be coming again."

The ground was white with frost, and Peter shivered as he stepped out of the cabin. Uncle Jim was taking the doe from the smokehouse. Peter looked at it and said, "We'd have had a fine buck, too, but for redskins."

"Might as well forget that," said Uncle Jim.

But Peter couldn't forget. Thinking about it made him feel hard inside. He went on across the clearing to open the pigpen. The thin black pigs crowded each other, eager to get out. "Take your time," he told them. "You've all day to root for acorns. Just mind you keep out of the way of wildcats and Indians."

When he followed Uncle Jim into the cabin for breakfast, Peter went to the corner and picked up the antlers. "When are we going to put these up?"

"Time enough for that," Uncle Jim told him. "There's work awaiting outside."

David, sitting at the table, asked, "Why does Mr. Dan put his head down and close his eyes and talk?"

"He's thanking God for the food," said Aunt Libby. "It's a good way to start the day." She looked at Uncle Jim.

He bowed his head and spoke a short prayer.

As Peter listened he grew quiet inside. But as soon as he opened his eyes, there were the antlers in the corner to remind him of his loss. Thinking of the buck, he didn't listen to Aunt Libby and Uncle Jim talking until he heard his name.

"Peter's been hankering to do some curing," Uncle Jim was saying.

"Hankering to cure my buck," said Peter quickly. "Aiming to do it alone." He swallowed hard. "Reckon I'll get me another some day." He glanced at Uncle Jim and said, "I could cure the doe real good."

David spoke up. "I'll hang the jerks in the sun."

"Keep the chip box full," Uncle Jim told him. "That's your job."

"I fetched chips yesterday," said David cheerfully. "Today I'll help Peter."

"You? Rub salt?" His mother smiled at him. "We have to be careful with it."

David slipped a piece of fried pumpkin from his bowl and dropped it on the floor for Nip. "I like salt," he said. "And so does Lady, and so does Belle."

"How do you know that?" asked Peter, grinning at him.

"'Cause they lick it," answered David. "Like this." His blue eyes sparkled as he licked his hand. "I gave them some, 'cause it's good for beasts."

"Beasts?" His mother repeated the word in a puzzled tone.

Mary Ann interrupted. "I remember! You were baking, and you spilled some salt on the table. And you said, 'Salt's good for man and beast.'"

"Oh yes," said Aunt Libby. She looked at David. "But I didn't give you any salt."

Uncle Jim frowned and asked, "Did you help yourself to the salt?"

David nodded his head. "I took it for Lady, and Belle wanted some too."

Uncle Jim turned to Peter. "Best get up and see how much he's taken."

As Peter climbed nimbly up the ladder, Aunt Libby said, "One gourd's near empty. The other should be full."

Peter felt his way to the gourds by the chimney. He put his hand and arm down inside the first gourd and felt a few grains of salt at the bottom. The other's the full one, he thought, and put in his fingers—then his hand and his arm. Way down he felt salt. Lifting the gourd, he found it wasn't heavy. He carried it to the ladder, and called down, "One's empty. Here's the other."

Uncle Jim came quickly and took the gourd while Peter stepped down. For a long moment Uncle Jim stared into the gourd, then carefully set it on the floor. His face had grown stern. There was no sound in the cabin, only the fire crackling. Looking at David, he said, "There's not much left. What did you do with the salt?"

David glanced from one to another. "Put it down by the creek, where Belle and Lady drink."

"David!" cried his mother. "Down by the creek? All that salt wasted!"

Head drooping, David backed away from her and the others toward the fireplace. "When I put the salt on the ground, it melted away."

"So you took more and more," murmured Peter, half under his breath. It was hard to believe.

Aunt Libby exclaimed, "That was what you were doing, going up and down the ladder with the broken gourd in your hand?"

"I saw him, too," said Mary Ann soberly. "I thought he was playing. I didn't guess he was helping himself to salt."

"How much have you for cooking?" asked Uncle Jim.

Aunt Libby looked into the small gourd hanging near the fireplace, and answered, "A few spoonfuls."

"We've enough in the big gourd to cure the skins today," Uncle Jim said slowly. "Not much over. It will be a fair spell afore I can get some more." He picked up his jacket.

"What ought we do to you?" Aunt Libby asked David.

Reckon something should be done to him, thought Peter. He looked at his small cousin. David was sobbing. Big tears rolled down his cheeks. Nip pressed close beside him and licked his hand.

Quickly Peter crossed the room, put his arm about David, and spoke to Uncle Jim. "He didn't know about salt. Reckon he won't be taking any more."

"Reckon not," said Uncle Jim, slipping on his jacket.

"Have we enough to keep our meat from spoiling?" asked Aunt Libby.

Uncle Jim shook his head. "We'll smoke what we can."

"No salt for breadmaking!" exclaimed Mary Ann.

"Nor for curing more skins," added Peter, thinking he might get another buck.

Uncle Jim left the cabin, and Peter followed him to watch the skinning of the doe. Carefully Peter spread the skin on the ground. He put stones around the edges, then pegged the skin down securely so it wouldn't shrink as it dried.

"I'll get the salt," said Uncle Jim. He came back carrying the large gourd. "Don't throw it on," he warned. "Take a little at a time and rub it in well. Make it go a long way. Don't waste any."

Peter nodded and knelt beside the skin. A few scraps of meat clung to it. With a sharp-edged stone he cleaned them off. Then he put a bit of salt on the skin and began to rub it in.

Tears forgotten, David came and squatted beside Peter. "Can't I rub salt too?" he begged.

"You'll get in my way," Peter told him. "Go throw sticks for Nip to chase," he suggested.

While Peter worked on the skin, Uncle Jim cut up the meat. Some of it he put in the smokehouse. The long thin strips of jerked meat he hung in the sun to dry.

As he skinned the raccoon, Uncle Jim remarked, "He's a big one. Mammy will make soft soap from the fat. Fur's pretty good, too," he added.

"We've a fair lot of furs," said Peter. "Where will you take them to trade? To Stanford?"

"More likely Shepherdsville," answered Uncle Jim. "They make salt there. I'll have to go sooner than I figured on."

Peter broke a lump of salt and pressed it into the skin.

"How's it going?" Uncle Jim asked, watching for a moment. "Want me to help some?"

"No," said Peter. His hands were red and stiff from the cold. The salt made them smart, but he could do it, and do it alone. Uncle Jim took his ax and went into the woods to cut down a tree, and David went with him.

In the cabin Aunt Libby was singing, teaching Mary Ann the words of the song, *O God Our Help in Ages Past.* Peter listened. He liked singing, theirs and Mr. Dan's, too. As he worked again on the skin, he thought of the story about the man who was wounded and the men who had wounded and robbed him. "Same as Indians," Peter said to himself. "That's what they do, steal horses and bucks and kill." He rubbed the skin harder, and muttered, "Redskins! They sure don't help anyone!"

At last the doeskin was finished. Peter looked at it proudly. Even Uncle Jim couldn't do it better, he decided. Then he glanced at the coonskin pegged nearby on the ground. That ought to be cured too. "Might as well start it," said Peter. It was slow work, and there wasn't much salt left. He was getting tired and wished Uncle Jim would come to help.

When Uncle Jim came back, the curing was just

about done. He rubbed his fingers over the skins and nodded. "You've done a right smart job," he said. "Any salt left?"

"Scraped bottom," answered Peter.

"I figured that," said Uncle Jim. "Well, let's peg the skins against the barn."

By the time that was done and the chores finished the day was over. In the cabin Peter picked up the antlers again, and asked, "Where can we put these?"

Aunt Libby turned from her cooking. "Those antlers? Put them over that shelf, where the fiddle and the Bible are. That's a fitting place for them."

Uncle Jim held them against the wall, and Aunt Libby said, "A bit lower. . . . Yes, that's the right spot."

Peter whittled pegs and Uncle Jim made holes in the logs to fit them. He hung the antlers on the pegs.

"They show up fine there," said Aunt Libby. "Now supper's ready."

Turkey leavings were good, but the corn bread, without salt, didn't taste right. David tried to feed his to Nip.

"Better eat it," his father told him. "We'll all be

missing salt for a while. We won't have any more until the weather breaks and I can go to trade skins."

There was something else they missed in the cabin that night. It was Mr. Dan. "I like hearing Mr. Dan read," said Mary Ann.

"Uncle Jim will read to us," said Aunt Libby. "Fetch him the Bible, Peter."

Uncle Jim put aside the pack saddle he was shaping from a hickory branch and lifted David to his knee. He opened the Book and began to read, about a boy named David, killing a giant called Goliath.

Peter watched his small cousin as he listened. David's eyes grew wider and wider. That's a good story, Peter decided. I wonder if I could learn to read it?

When the story ended, David said, "I could kill a giant."

Aunt Libby laughed, and Mary Ann remarked, "Ain't no giants hereabouts."

"Might be some redskins," suggested Peter.

"Hope none of them come around here," said Aunt Libby quickly.

"I reckon," Uncle Jim spoke thoughtfully, "after that horse raid they'll keep out of sight for a spell."

Aunt Libby, David, and Mary Ann went to bed. But Peter crouched close to the fire. He held the Book open toward the light to read the letters he knew. Uncle Jim sat by him and taught him some of the words. When the fire burned low, they, too, went to bed.

Letters and words flickered like shadows before Peter's closed eyes. He hugged himself under the covers and whispered, "I'm learning to read. I'll be teaching my sister, and David, too, when he's older."

CHAPTER 7

Preparing for a Journey

As the weeks went by, there was little time to read during the daylight hours. Peter was hauling and chopping wood. And he was helping Uncle Jim clear ground to make the cornfield larger. They'd been working at it, on and off, a good part of the winter. Now spring was coming, and they had to ready the field for planting.

On their way to the cabin one day, Peter and Uncle Jim stopped in the woods to look at some maples. Sap oozed from holes where the trees had been tapped before.

"Everything comes sudden-like in spring," remarked Uncle Jim. "Sugar time, ploughing, and planting."

"Aunt Libby and I could do the sugaring," suggested Peter.

When they talked it over with her, she said, "Have to keep the fire going under the kettle. Boiling sap takes a sight of wood."

Uncle Jim looked at Peter. "Think you can chop enough and tote the buckets?"

Peter nodded eagerly.

The next morning Uncle Jim bored small holes in the trees. Into them Peter put the little tubes carved from cane. Below the tubes he hung buckets to catch the sap as it dripped.

"I can do something," said David, tagging after Peter. "I'll help, and Nip too."

"Watch the buckets," said his father. "When they're near full call Peter. He'll tote them to the kettle."

The fire started, Peter was splitting wood when he heard barking. He turned quickly. There was David, lugging a bucket. Sap was spilling over and dripping on his clothes. Nip raced around him and jumped against him, trying to pull the coontail swinging from David's cap.

"Down, Nip!" Peter shouted. "Down!" He dropped the ax.

"I'll tote that bucket," he called out, and ran toward David, hand outstretched to take it.

With a sharp bark Nip jumped hard against David's back. He tumbled over against Peter, knocked him backward, and put the sap bucket upside down in his lap.

"Ugh!" grunted Peter, the breath knocked out of him. Sap spread in a dark sticky patch over his shirt and breeches. "You and your help!" he cried, when he got his breath.

"Nip didn't mean it," said David, getting up.

Looking down at himself, Peter groaned. "See what you've done? I'm sticky sap all over!" For a moment he felt like throwing the empty bucket at Nip, or David, or maybe both of them. Slowly he got up and hung the bucket back on the tree.

Other buckets were getting full. He took one and, holding it away from his clothes, brought it to the kettle. David and Nip trailed after him.

When Mary Ann saw Peter she stared, then began to laugh. "You're . . . you're sap all over!"

Aunt Libby glanced at him and smiled. "We'll have to put you in the sugar kettle. What happened?" she asked.

David spoke up in a teary voice. "We did it. Nip and me. We were helping."

"Helping!" exclaimed Peter, looking at the small boy. David had rubbed his eyes with his sticky hands. There were tear tracks through the dirt on his face and streaks of sap on his shirt and breeches. Nip stood close beside him, holding David's cap in his mouth.

"You're a fine helping pair," said Peter. Then, in spite of himself, he began to grin. "Reckon you'd best put us both in the kettle," he said to Aunt Libby.

"There's sap enough and to spare," she said, with a smile. "Fetch the other buckets while I get out your other shirts and old breeches, if you can get into them." She smiled again. "Both of you've growed some this past year."

While sugar making went on Uncle Jim worked in the field. Every few days he hunted for meat—turkey, rabbit, or squirrel. There was no salt to keep meat from spoiling or to cure skins.

Often in the evening Uncle Jim molded bullets and Peter helped. "We've made a heap of them," he remarked one evening.

"It takes a sight for hunting," Uncle Jim told him. "You'll be needing them, when I go off."

"We'll need plenty, too," added Mary Ann, "if redskins come round."

Besides molding bullets in the evenings, Peter helped to make brooms. Uncle Jim fetched home hickory saplings and showed him how to split one end of each sapling into fine, strawlike parts, then tie them with a thong.

And there was corn seed to get ready for planting. Uncle Jim spread a cloth on the floor. From the loft he brought the full ears of corn he had saved for seed. All of them, excepting David, helped to sort the ears and shell them. Sometimes, while the others worked, Aunt Libby took Mr. Dan's Book and read to them.

Then, when the others had gone to bed, Peter sat near the firelight, learning new words. Often it was hard to keep his eyes open. One night he fell asleep. Starting awake, he heard Aunt Libby speaking.

"When do you plan to go?" she was asking.

"Soon as I've got the seed in," answered Uncle Jim. "Got to do that, or we'll be out of corn afore the next crop is ready."

"Nothing tastes right any more," said Aunt Libby. "The young'uns are getting thin. David hardly eats anything."

"Reckon he won't waste salt again," said Uncle Jim.

Aunt Libby sighed. "We'll never forget the need of it."

None of us will forget, Peter thought soberly, as he put the Book on the shelf and went to his bed.

It was another week before the planting was done. Then the furs were taken out, aired, and tied into bundles.

"I'm off for Shepherdsville, come morning," said Uncle Jim.

No one wanted to go to bed that night. At last Peter and Uncle Jim were left alone, sitting near the fire. "It'll be up to you to look after things while I'm gone," Uncle Jim told Peter. "There's plenty of shot and powder for the two guns here, yours and the old one Aunt Libby can handle, if she needs to." His tone was grave and quiet.

Peter nodded. A heaviness seemed to be settling on his shoulders.

"You'll have to hunt some," said Uncle Jim. 'And keep watch of the cornfield. Crows will be around, after the seed. Don't waste your bullets shooting them. Use sticks and stones. And keep an eye on David. He's apt to go looking for a giant." Uncle Jim's eyes twinkled.

He's trying to cheer me up, thought Peter. "How long you aiming for to be gone?" he asked.

"Might be ten days or so," answered Uncle Jim. "I'll get back fast as I can."

"Wish you were heading home, 'stead of starting," said Peter in a low voice. He hadn't minded Uncle Jim's going before. Then it was only for a few days. This time, somehow, his going seemed different.

It was late when Peter went to the loft. He meant to be up early, but when he awoke the next morning Uncle Jim was gone.

"I'll be right glad when he's back," said Aunt Libby. She carried the bedcovers out to air in the spring sunshine.

"We'll be glad for some salt, too," added Mary Ann.

That night when David and Mary Ann had gone to bed, Aunt Libby and Peter sat by the fire. He was trying to read, but it was hard to keep his mind on the words for thinking about Uncle Jim. Aunt Libby kept turning her head to listen. Twice she asked, "Sure you latched the barn?"

"Sure did," Peter told her.

"I wonder how far Jim got today," she said softly.

"How far is it to Shepherdsville?" asked Peter.

"Sixty-five, maybe seventy miles," answered Aunt Libby. "He may go on to Louisville, if it's better trading there." She got up and walked back and forth, and tried the latch on the door. "Let's pray he'll get back safely."

Aunt Libby and Peter knelt by their stools, but no words came. After a few moments she whispered, "Amen." Standing up she put her arm across Peter's shoulders. "Now I feel better. God will look after Jim."

Peter nodded. He couldn't speak for the lump in his throat.

Uncle Jim had chopped a pile of wood before leaving, but it burned quickly. In a few days, when the pile was getting low, Peter was up early to chop some more. Suddenly he heard cawing. Like a drift of black soot from the chimney, blown by the wind, a flock of birds passed overhead. "Crows!" he cried out.

"Run, Peter," Aunt Libby called to him. "They'll be after the seed. I'll do the chores."

Peter ran, but the crows flew faster. They were busy digging up seed when he reached the field. He shouted and threw stones at them. With a rush of black wings the birds flew into the nearby trees.

Cawing, as though they were laughing, they sat and watched Peter walk back and forth. "If I step out of sight," he told them, "I know you'll be back in a hurry scratching."

After a while David came, bringing pieces of fried pumpkin and some dry corn bread. Peter sat down under an old oak tree to rest and eat. Soon a shiny blackbird dropped boldly into the far corner of the field. Another, and another followed.

"Birds!" cried David, pointing. Peter jumped up. He and David chased crows until they were out of breath.

"Reckon they think we're birds and chasing them is a game," said Peter. Flapping his arms, like wings, he cawed back at the crows. David laughed, then flapped his arms and cawed too.

At first it was fun. But the sun was hot, and they grew tired and thirsty. They had to keep watching, or the birds would come back.

"Fetch a piggin of water from the cabin," Peter suggested.

It seemed a long time before David brought it. "Mammy says come home when the birds go to sleep," he told Peter.

"They won't nest till sundown," said Peter. He was warm and tired.

When it was almost dark, they trudged back to the cabin. David drank some milk, but pushed away his bowl of stew. "I can't chew this meat," he said.

"Jerked meat is tough," said his mother, "even though I soaked this a long time. Try these spring greens Mary Ann gathered."

"We'd have cured meat," said Mary Ann severely, "if we had some salt."

"Can't keep food without it," murmured Aunt Libby. She turned to Peter. "Perhaps tomorrow you could hunt for a spell and get some fresh meat. Mary Ann and David could watch the field."

Resting his head on his hand, David sighed. "I chased lots and lots of crows today."

"I know," said his mother smiling at him. "But there will be more to chase tomorrow."

CHAPTER 8

Mr. Dan Comes Again

THE next morning Peter went hunting. The woods
were full of spring smells. Flowers were pushing
up through old, dead leaves, and oaks were tassel-
ing out. Redbirds, robins, and warblers were singing, fit to burst their throats. They stopped when
Peter came near, then sang again when he had
passed.

Peter walked for an hour before he heard a
rustling sound under a clump of bushes. His keen

eyes saw something brown stir. "Rabbit," he murmured, and quickly aimed and fired.

As Peter ran to pick it up, another rabbit scurried away. "Two of them, there were. Should've got them both," he told himself.

Carefully Peter reloaded his gun and walked on, watching and listening. After a while he shot another rabbit. Two will be enough, he decided. We've no salt to keep them. Reckon I'd best turn back.

"Maybe David will eat some stew," said Aunt Libby, hopefully, when she took the rabbits from Peter.

At sundown he was fetching water from the brook when there was a shout nearby. A big dappled gray horse stood beside the fence. The circuit rider had come. Peter dashed to open the bars. "Uncle Jim's away," he told Mr. Dan breathlessly. "Gone to trade skins."

"You'll have supper with us and stay the night?" asked Aunt Libby.

Mr. Dan smiled. "I'll have some supper and rest for a few hours in the barn. I'm off my circuit. When the moon comes up, I'll find my way back to the trail without disturbing you."

It was good to have Mr. Dan around. He took

care of his horse and chopped wood. "Swinging an ax gives a man a wonderful appetite," he said, when Aunt Libby called him to eat.

"We've rabbit stew," she said. "Hope you like bay leaves. I put them in for flavor." She didn't say there was no salt.

Fresh meat was easier to chew than jerked meat. Mr. Dan ate as if he liked everything, even the dry corn bread. David watched him and ate when he saw Mr. Dan eating.

After supper, looking at Peter and smiling, Mr. Dan said, "I wanted to come this way, because I have something—strings for that violin of yours." He took them from his pocket.

Peter sucked in a long breath. Quickly he brought the fiddle. He watched closely while the strings were put on and tightened until they were in tune.

Mr. Dan played a few notes, and then he played the song he had sung before, *O God Our Help in Ages Past.* A lump swelled in Peter's throat as he listened. His father's fiddle, playing again! His fingers itched to make it sing.

"Let me give you a lesson," said Mr. Dan, handing the fiddle to Peter. He showed him how to hold it under his chin, and press the strings with his fingers. Guiding Peter's hand, he moved the bow across the strings.

Peter tried it alone and looked up, disappointed. It sounded so different, scratchy and harsh.

"When you have learned to play, it won't be like that," Mr. Dan told him, smiling. "A violin sings without words. It can speak thoughts that are deep in the heart."

"My pappy played like that," said Peter softly. "I remember. I'm going to play like him."

"I don't know how we can thank you," said Aunt Libby. Her voice sounded shaky. "I used to play a bit myself. Reckon I can help Peter."

"I'm learning to read, too," Peter told Mr. Dan. "And I'm going to teach Mary Ann."

"That's a fine idea," said Mr. Dan heartily. Sitting down, he took out his Bible, opened it, and read. He prayed, too, asking God to take care of them and Uncle Jim. Then he tucked his Book in his saddlebag and picked up his cloak. "It's time to say good night and good-by."

Peter wished Mr. Dan could stay longer. "I'll walk to the barn with you," he said. "I'll fix you a bed."

"You could sleep in the barn, along with Mr.

Dan," Aunt Libby suggested. "Fetch some covers from the loft."

"That's too much trouble," Mr. Dan protested. "I'm used to sleeping. . . ."

Aunt Libby interrupted. "I know, you're used to sleeping under a bush or a rock, in snow or in rain."

Mr. Dan smiled and shook his head.

Peter brought skins from the loft. At the door he paused, stepped back, and took his gun. In the barn, he threw down some stalks, and Mr. Dan helped to spread the skins over them; then he lay down and drew his long cloak over his shoulders.

Peter latched the barn door and stretched himself on the bed he had made. Carefully he placed his gun on the floor beside him. "Uncle Jim says, always keep your gun loaded and where you can reach it," he remarked. "Never know when redskins might come. They've killed lots of settlers."

"Yes," said Mr. Dan. "Yes, I know."

In a low, hard voice Peter said, "I saw them kill my pappy."

"You saw them!" exclaimed Mr. Dan. "Do you want to tell me about it?"

Peter did want to tell Mr. Dan. Maybe then he'd

understand about redskins and not be so soft. But it was hard to begin. "It was when we were moving to Kentucky," he began at last. "We were coming along with other settlers, more than fifty of them, I reckon. We rode, single file, along the trail. Wilderness Road they call it."

"I know that road," said Mr. Dan. "Of course someone, a guide who knew the way, was leading the party?"

"A scout," Peter told him. "A few of the other men knew the way, too. Some of them rode up front and some at the end of the line. They wouldn't let anyone ride off alone, or lag behind, or get out of line. Uncle Jim and Aunt Libby were up front. David was a baby. Mary Ann and my mammy were there, too." Peter paused and swallowed. "My pappy was near the end. I rode behind him, on his big black horse.

"At first folks were singing happy-like as they went along," said Peter. "Then, towards the end, nobody sang or even talked much. They just kept going." He remembered the smell of dry dust, the sound of thudding horses' hoofs, and the squeaking of packs and of leather saddles.

"Yes," Mr. Dan prompted quietly.

Peter took a deep breath. "Reckon folks were

getting tired. At sundown some of them were for making camp. But the scout and my pappy said, no. They were afraid Indians were following our trail. We wouldn't be safe, they said, not till we got to Crab Orchard."

Peter stopped again, and Mr. Dan asked, "Did you reach Crab Orchard that night?"

"Some did," answered Peter. "Just about dark the redskins came up behind us. They yelled and began shooting guns and arrows. Pappy said, 'Drop off and keep out of sight.' I slid from his horse and crawled under some bushes."

In a low voice he went on, "When I looked out, I saw him throw up his arm. His gun went flying into the weeds, and he fell. A redskin took his horse."

Talking about it made his throat hurt. Peter swallowed hard and stared into the darkness. He remembered just how it was. He pressed his hands over his ears to shut out the memory of women and children screaming, horses stampeding, redskins all around close, and everyone else riding away from him fast, leaving him alone.

"They . . . they thought I was killed," he explained, "along with my pappy. In the dark the Indians didn't see me. They didn't scalp me. They

went back into the woods. I heard them in the night, signaling like owls. When it was dark and still, I crawled out from the bushes and found Pappy's gun. Found Pappy, too," he added. "He was dead . . . scalped. I sat by him all the night."

"The others?" asked Mr. Dan quietly. "Did they reach Crab Orchard safely?"

"Most of them," answered Peter. "My mammy and some of them got wounded. Next morning Uncle Jim and settlers from Crab Orchard came and found me. They buried my pappy and three other men there." Peter brushed his hand across his moist eyes. "Mammy died, too, in a few days. Aunt Libby says it was mostly from grieving over Pappy."

Suddenly, sitting up and clutching his gun, Peter said in a hard voice, "Now you know why I'm for killing redskins, all of them!"

There was no sound in the barn for a moment. Then Mr. Dan asked, "If you kill them, will that make anything right? Will it make your folks live again?"

Peter answered slowly, "Reckon not. But they have it coming." Didn't the circuit rider understand? Did Mr. Dan like redskins? Peter lay down again and stared into the darkness. The question bothered him until he burst out, "You don't . . . don't have a liking for them, do you?"

"I don't like all the things they have done," answered Mr. Dan. "But I'm sure killing won't help. We must try to understand how they feel. This was their land. Settlers have come and taken it. They have killed off the game that Indians depended on for food. How would you feel, if you were an Indian?"

"I'm not an Indian," Peter muttered. "I still don't like them."

"We don't approve of everything they do," Mr. Dan spoke with firmness. "But there are good Indians, I know."

Peter lay still, thinking over what Mr. Dan had said. Were there good Indians? First he'd have to see one.

When Mr. Dan stood up, Peter got up too.

"Did I wake you?" asked Mr. Dan.

"Wasn't sleeping," answered Peter.

"The moon is up, and I must be on my way," said Mr. Dan. He carried his saddlebags into Silver Boy's stall.

Peter walked to the fence with Mr. Dan and his horse. "You'll be coming back?" he asked.

"Yes," answered Mr. Dan. "In five or six

weeks probably, the Lord willing." He rode away through the silvery light.

Peter watched until the circuit rider was out of sight. A whippoorwill sang a few sleepy notes, and he shivered. Back in the barn, he locked the door, lay down and fell asleep, his hand on his gun.

"Peter, Peter!" Aunt Libby's voice roused him next morning.

When he opened the door, she said, "I've sent Mary Ann and David to chase crows. Help yourself to breakfast while I milk Belle."

CHAPTER 9

David's Adventure

HALF-ASLEEP, Peter plodded to the cabin. Deep inside of him the words Mr. Dan had spoken echoed. Peter shook his head, as though to get rid of them.

After breakfast, while he was chopping wood, he thought again of what Mr. Dan had said. Stopping for a moment, he rested the ax against his knee and pushed his hair up under his cap. Reckon God doesn't like everything we do, Peter thought soberly. He lifted the ax again, swung it, and brought it down hard, splitting a piece of wood in

91

two. God loves Indians, Mr. Dan says, but I don't, and I don't aim to have any part of them either.

Mr. Dan had been gone for several days and Uncle Jim for more than a week. The rabbit stew had been eaten. Now, again, there was only jerked meat and bread without salt. When David pushed his bowl away, Aunt Libby said, "You mustn't waste food." She sighed and put her arms on the table, resting her head on them.

Peter looked at her anxiously. She's weary, he thought, and misses Uncle Jim. If she had something different to cook, maybe that would help some.

When Peter climbed down from the loft the next morning, Aunt Libby was sitting at the table, reading Mr. Dan's Book. "You're up early," she said.

"Aim to go hunting, soon as the chores get done," said Peter. It was midafternoon before he brought home a turkey gobbler.

"It would taste a sight better if. . . ." Aunt Libby began, and then pressed her lips tightly together.

If we had salt, thought Peter.

"Mary Ann and David are watching the field," said Aunt Libby. "Send Mary Ann back to pluck this bird. I'm cleaning the cabin."

Peter found Mary Ann alone. "Where's David?" he asked.

"He traipsed to the cabin long ago," she answered.

"Didn't see him," said Peter. "Aunt Libby wants you."

"I haven't seen a crow in a long while," said Mary Ann, as she started for home.

Peter turned his head to look and listen. No crows? How still everything was. Birds always stop chirping when someone comes along, he reasoned. Then his heart skipped a beat. Slowly he dropped down, as though he were going to sleep. Quickly he rolled over, wormed his way under some bushes, waited and listened. Soon he heard someone calling. Then there were footsteps. Someone running!

"Peter! Peter!" It was Mary Ann calling. He slid from his hiding place.

"It's . . . it's David!" she gasped. "Don't know where he's gone. Aunt Libby hasn't seen him."

Crows forgotten, Peter raced ahead of Mary Ann back to the cabin. Where was David? Had he wandered off, gotten lost?

"I called and called," said Aunt Libby, a catch in her voice. "He might be hiding somewheres."

"And . . . gone . . . asleep," gasped Mary Ann, still breathless from running.

Peter's heart was thumping from his run. He took his gun and promised, "I'll find him. Nip's with him. They'll leave a trail." Looking at Aunt Libby's white face, he added, "Might be he's gone hunting for a giant."

"You're a comfort, Peter," said Aunt Libby, trying to smile.

Peter searched for David around the barn and the loft, in the smokehouse, and in the springhouse. He walked along the fence and poked in all the nooks where David might creep to hide or to play. But David was nowhere around.

Peter stopped to think where to look next. David had been with Mary Ann at the cornfield. I'd best look there for his trail, Peter decided. As he hurried toward the field he remembered the silent birds and caught his breath. Had someone, a redskin, been near, put his hand over David's mouth, and carried him off? Peter shivered and gripped his gun hard.

There was a trail from the cornfield to the brook. David might have gone there. Looking for signs, Peter went that way. But there was no small boy, or hound dog, in the woods or at the brook.

With eyes and ears sharpened by fear, Peter walked toward the place where the cane grew thick and tall. If David had got into the cane, he'd never find his way out. More than once Uncle Jim had warned him not to hide in there. If only Uncle Jim were home! He'd know what to do, which way to go. Or Mr. Dan might help. But what could he do? The circuit rider would pray. I could do that, Peter decided.

Pausing for a moment, he closed his eyes. "Please help me find little David," he prayed, then hurried along.

Far off he thought he heard a dog bark faintly. The sound seemed to come from down near the trail that led past the hill. Could David have walked that far? Then Peter heard another bark, more clearly. That's Nip, for sure, he told himself. He began to run as fast as he could. Another bark, louder, this time . . . and nearer. Then between the trees Peter saw Nip. He was tugging at something on the ground. It was David!

Peter was out of breath when he knelt beside the small boy. "Are you all right?" he gasped. "Stop, Nip! You've torn his jacket."

David opened his eyes, and said in a tired voice, "Nip didn't do it, the wildcat did."

"Wildcat!" exclaimed Peter, looking around. "Where?"

Slowly David sat up and pointed downhill toward a large tree.

Peter stared at the small boy. Was it true, or was David making up a story? "How did you happen to see a wildcat?" he asked.

"Nip saw it. He barked," answered David. "I was going to shoot it with this." He held up a stick about the shape of a gun. "But it jumped and caught me, like this." David grabbed the torn

shoulder of his jacket with one hand. "I fell down,"
he added. "And then the Indian shot it."

"Indian!" whispered Peter. Quickly he was on
his feet, his gun held ready. A chill crept over him
as he looked sharply at the nearby trees.

"The Indian helped me up," said David.

Still glancing watchfully around, Peter asked
quietly, "Where's the wildcat?"

"He took it, the Indian. That way," answered
David, pointing to the trail leading south. "I
walked some, but I can't walk any more."

Peter thought for a moment. I'd best look around, he decided. "Rest here," he said to David. "I'll be back right soon. Nip, stay here," he ordered.

Alert to the movement of every leaf and twig and to every sound, Peter walked in the direction David had pointed. Under a big tree he stopped. Above him was the branch where the wildcat had been. Below it, the picture was clear. The ground was scuffed where the animal had jumped and where David had fallen. There were footprints, too, moccasin footprints.

Peter followed them a little way. The Indian was moving along to the south. No use trailing him. He hurried back to David. "You shouldn't have gone wandering," Peter told David soberly. "That wildcat could have killed you. I'm glad the redskin got it."

"He's a good Indian," said David.

"Mr. Dan said there were good ones," said Peter. "We'll tell him about it, when he comes. Now let's be getting home."

It was a long way uphill to the cabin. David tried to walk, but his steps lagged. Peter put his arm around him to help, but David moved more and more slowly. "Walk faster," urged Peter.

David tried, and stumbled. "My legs won't go," he said.

"You can't stay here," said Peter. Rubbing his chin the way Uncle Jim often did, he wondered what to do. "Got my gun to carry," he said. "How can I tote you?" He took a deep breath. "Reckon I've got to try."

Stooping, he said, "Climb up on my shoulders, and hang on tight."

He staggered with the extra load. It was hard to walk. When they came in sight of the clearing he was glad. Nip ran ahead, barking. Aunt Libby and Mary Ann heard him and came hurrying to meet Peter and David.

"Where did you find him?" Aunt Libby asked Peter. There were glad tears in her eyes as she lifted David from Peter's back. "You've torn your jacket!" she exclaimed to David. "Now how did you do that?"

"He's not hurt any," Peter told her. "Found him way down yonder, near the big trail."

Aunt Libby held David close. "Why did you go?" she asked.

"To find my pappy," he answered, struggling to free himself. "He's bringing some salt." He closed his eyes and sighed. "I'm right tired."

"Plain tuckered out," murmured his mother. When they reached the cabin she put him on her bed. Peter sat down beside David and told them about the wildcat and the Indian.

"He's a good Indian," murmured David half asleep.

"He might have fetched you home," said Mary Ann.

"No!" exclaimed Peter sharply. "We don't want a redskin nosing round here, and Uncle Jim away."

"I've heard Indians are kind to young'uns," said Aunt Libby thoughtfully. "Perhaps he thought Jim was somewheres near." She paused, then stepped to the door to fasten the latch. "We don't know what the Indian was thinking. It's spring and some of them may be roaming about to hunt, or to raid. We'll be watching out for them."

"I wish Uncle Jim would get here soon," said Mary Ann in a low voice.

CHAPTER 10

Uncle Jim's Return

AFTER supper Peter took the Bible from the shelf and said, "I'm going to read some."

"Let's read together," suggested Aunt Libby.

Peter and Mary Ann moved their stools close beside hers. Aunt Libby turned the pages of the Book, Peter read aloud, and Mary Ann looked and listened. Soon they knew the words by heart. "We'll surprise Jim when he comes," said Aunt Libby.

But several days passed, and he did not come. Peter was finding it hard to sleep. He kept remembering what he had heard—stories of wild animals in the woods, and Indians. How now and again a man was found near a trail, scalped, or with an arrow in his back. Sometimes Indians caught a man alone and carried him off a prisoner. If only he knew where Uncle Jim was . . . and that he was safe! The cornhusks of his bed rustled as he twisted and turned.

"What's the matter, Peter?" Aunt Libby called up to him. "Go to sleep."

"She's not sleeping either," Peter said to himself.

The first thing in the morning and often during the day Aunt Libby was at the door, her eyes searching the woods. She's looking for Uncle Jim, thought Peter. I'm watching for him, too.

A couple of days later the sky darkened, and it began to rain. It rained softly that day and the next one. And Uncle Jim had been gone for two weeks. "There's no sense going to the cornfield in this rain," said Aunt Libby. "Everything's soaking."

Rain pelted against Peter's face as he ran to the barn to do the chores. It dripped down his neck when he went out for wood. When he carried in an armful and put it on the hearth, he sat by the fire to get dry.

"We needed this rain," remarked Aunt Libby. "Now the corn will sprout fast."

"And then squirrels will come to dig it up," said Mary Ann, as she pounded corn, making corn meal.

Peter poked at the fire. "Come crows or squirrels, what do they matter," he said, and added to himself, "if only Uncle Jim would get here."

Nip dozed near the fire. "Lazy hound dog," said Peter, stooping to scratch his back. Nip opened one eye and twitched his ears. A moment later he lifted his head, jumped up, ran to the door and out into the rain.

"Jim's coming!" cried Aunt Libby. "Nip knows!"

Peter started for the door, but Aunt Libby brushed past him. "I see Lady! He's home!" Half laughing and half crying, she twisted her apron front to back, pulled it over her head, and hurried out in the rain to meet him.

Mary Ann and Peter ran, too. And David, shouting, "My pappy's come!" trotted after them as fast as his short legs could go.

When Uncle Jim had hugged each one, Peter

gave a deep sigh. "I was wondering if you'd ever get here."

"It was slow and slippery, walking in rain and mud," said Uncle Jim. "Lady dropped a shoe. Had to go back a way and get it fixed."

The packsaddle on Lady's back was piled high. Uncle Jim led her to the cabin to unload. There was wool for Aunt Libby, needles and thread, and a big black kettle and some gunpowder.

"What's in this big sack?" asked Mary Ann.

"Potatoes, for seed," answered Uncle Jim. "I figured we could use this, too." He set a sharp, shiny ax against the cabin. Then, handing Peter a square black thing with a wooden frame, he warned, "Be careful of this. It could break."

"A slate!" exclaimed Aunt Libby. "So you can learn to write."

David tugged at his father's jacket. "Did you fetch some salt?"

His father swung him high up to his shoulder. "Sure did! A big leather sack of it."

"Let me taste some!" begged David.

Aunt Libby laughed. "Everything will taste good now."

" 'Cause Uncle Jim's home," said Peter, nodding. "Having you here is just as good as having salt."

"Better than salt," said Aunt Libby, putting her face close to Uncle Jim's arm. "Because we love him."

David, Mary Ann, and Peter all tried to talk at the same time. They wanted to tell about the crows and the circuit rider's visit; about David, the wildcat, and the Indian. "He was a good Indian," David insisted.

Peter admitted, "Could be there's a good one."

Uncle Jim listened and nodded gravely.

While they talked, Aunt Libby hummed softly. She did her best for supper. The jerked meat was cut into tiny pieces and stewed a long time. She went out in the rain and gathered some mustard greens to cook. Mary Ann made corn bread and put in some salt.

When David had finished eating, he sat back on his stool with a satisfied grunt. Then he left his place to sit on his father's knee.

"Tell us, where did you go?" asked Peter.

"Followed our creek till I struck the trail through the hills," said Uncle Jim. Looking at Aunt Libby, he added, "Saw mighty fine evergreen trees on those hills. Cedars of Lebanon, they call them. Folks are settling through there, on toward Springfield. Some named Hardin, and some Wickliffe."

"Did you stay the night with them?" asked Aunt Libby.

"No," answered Uncle Jim. "I headed for Shepherdsville. Got there the second night. Stayed a few days."

"Where they make salt," added Peter.

David reached up his hand and touched his father's face. "I could make salt."

"No," said his father sternly. "And you're not taking the new kettle, or an old one, to the creek for to try it."

"Did you trade our furs at Shepherdsville?" asked Peter.

"No," answered Uncle Jim. "Figured I'd do better at Louisville."

"Tell us about Louisville," Mary Ann broke in eagerly. "What's there?"

"It's a growing place," said Uncle Jim. "Must be near three hundred folks living there . . . besides traders and settlers coming and going."

Peter took a deep breath. "That's a heap of folks!"

"And some soldiers there, too, aren't there?" asked Aunt Libby. "And a fort to look out for settlers?"

Uncle Jim nodded. "Fort Nelson, built fifteen

years ago, or thereabouts. When Indians were stirred up bad and were crossing the river."

"They're still crossing over," remarked Aunt Libby.

"For raids, like the one Mr. Dan nearly got caught in," added Peter.

"Now and again they cross over," Uncle Jim agreed. "But mostly they're after loaded flatboats going downriver."

To take what isn't theirs, thought Peter, remembering his buck. He glanced at the antlers and clenched his fists. "If they come this way," his voice was sharp, "we'd fight them. I'd shoot fast!"

"Hope they won't come," said Uncle Jim. "We aim to live peaceably with them, if they'll let us." He looked down at David, dozing in his arms, and added quietly, "Could be there are some redskins folks needn't be afraid of."

"Like the Indian that saved David," said Mary Ann.

Uncle Jim cleared his throat and said, in a different tone of voice, "It wasn't Indians kept me awake all night up there in Louisville."

"What was it?" asked Mary Ann quickly.

"Singing," answered Uncle Jim gravely. "Singing all the night."

"Singing?" said Aunt Libby looking puzzled. "All night?"

Uncle Jim nodded. "From those ponds around town," he said, his eyes beginning to twinkle. "The frogs kept croaking the livelong night." He winked at Peter and Mary Ann.

They laughed, and Aunt Libby said, "Jim Rowan! That's enough. We're all getting to bed right off."

CHAPTER 11

Tall Corn

RAIN helped the tender green spears of corn to grow quickly. Weeds in the field sprang up as fast as the corn. Peter and Uncle Jim hoed them out and drew the soil into little hills around the corn to keep the stalks growing straight. Peter helped to plant potatoes, pumpkins, cabbage, and turnips. Aunt Libby and Mary Ann planted gourd seeds.

The days grew warmer and, in the evenings, while it was still light, the whole family stayed out of doors. Peter and Mary Ann sat under the big tree near the house. They were learning words in

Mr. Dan's book and took turns writing on their slate. David played with Nip.

When the light faded Aunt Libby would say to Peter, "Fetch out the fiddle. You don't need to see for feeling the strings." She was helping him learn to play the song Mr. Dan liked to sing. Sometimes she sang other songs.

"You're doing better every time," Aunt Libby told him. "Mr. Dan will be surprised when he comes."

"I've been looking for the circuit rider," said Uncle Jim. "He hasn't been around for a spell . . . not since I was away. I'd like to see him."

Peter spoke quickly. "He said he'd be back in five or six weeks."

"Weeks go fast," remarked Aunt Libby, looking thoughtful. "It's more than six weeks."

"Could be he's riding another circuit, or maybe stopped riding," said Uncle Jim.

"Circuiting's a hard way of life," said Aunt Libby. "Half the time not getting enough to eat, and sleeping out when night comes on."

Mary Ann spoke up. "And riding alone, through the wilderness, with Indians raiding and wildcats about."

Peter's fingers gripped the violin tightly. Indians,

wildcats, and other animals! Something could happen, but to Mr. Dan? He caught his breath. Not to him!

"He'll come," said Peter in a low voice. "I know he'll come." Deep within himself he added, as he carried the violin into the cabin, "He's sure to come. Wildcats or Indians won't get him. God wouldn't let them."

He kept thinking about Mr. Dan during the next few days. He looked up often, expecting to see Silver Boy or hear hoofbeats.

"We're needing meat," said Aunt Libby.

"Peter will get something," said Uncle Jim. And the next afternoon, Peter took his gun and went into the woods.

Swinging his gun back and forth, Peter walked awhile without seeing anything to shoot at. Then he got a fat possum. Gun reloaded, he turned homeward, taking the way around the other side of the hill, hoping to get something more.

Birds were beginning their evening songs and, inside himself, Peter was singing along with them. The afternoon sun shone between the trees. Shading his eyes with his hand, he glanced down and stopped short. In the ground before him was the plain mark of a horse's hoof!

A happy thought flashed into his mind. Mr. Dan and Silver Boy were coming at last! Peter took a few eager steps and paused again. Clearly, beside the hoofprint, were the marks of a foot in the moist ground. He bent down to look more closely.

"Someone wearing moccasins," Peter whispered, "turning in his toes, the way Indians do."

Like a sudden cold wind a chill crept over him. Not Mr. Dan, but an Indian was coming, leading a horse. Peter straightened up and looked around sharply. I must see him, he decided, and find out where he's heading. He hung the possum from a branch, as high as he could reach, for he could go faster without it. Then, gun in both hands, ready to aim and fire quickly, he cautiously followed the footprints.

After some distance, through the trees ahead, he glimpsed a tall, dappled gray horse. Silver Boy! Peter was about to shout, "Mr. Dan!" Instead he gripped his gun and held his breath.

Someone wearing buckskins and moccasins held the horse's bridle. For a moment Peter saw the side of an Indian's face and dark hair streaked with gray. Where was Mr. Dan?

Peter could hardly breathe. What had happened? Had the Indian killed Mr. Dan? Killed and scalped him, as they had scalped his father? Suddenly deep, hot anger rushed through Peter. "I'll get him, that redskin!" he told himself grimly, and shivered as he raised his gun to aim.

The horse kept swishing his tail and pawing the ground. And Peter's hands shook. "Don't hit Silver Boy," he told himself, and bit his lips until it hurt. Holding himself tightly, he waited for a chance to shoot.

The Indian moved. One side of his head showed. Quickly the shrill crack of a rifle broke the quiet of the woods as Peter fired.

The Indian slumped forward and lay on the ground. Silver Boy reared and pranced. Peter ran and caught his bridle, then turned to look at the Indian.

Everything was hushed. The birds had stopped twittering. The leaves were still. "He's . . . he's dead," whispered Peter slowly. "I did it!" The hot angry feeling was gone, but he had a queer, upset feeling in his stomach. He stared and backed away from the limp figure on the ground, wishing the old Indian would move.

A twig cracked. Someone was coming down the hill in a hurry. Peter gripped his empty gun and waited.

It was a tall man, with a long black cloak. The circuit rider! "Mr. Dan!" Peter's voice trembled as he called out. "Mr. Dan, this redskin was taking your horse. I shot him."

The circuit rider didn't seem to hear. He hurried to the Indian and knelt beside him. Lifting the Indian's head, he wiped the blood from the side of it with his kerchief and examined it with great care.

Churned inside, puzzled, and a little frightened, Peter watched Mr. Dan and the Indian.

"A scalp wound," Mr. Dan murmured. "Knocked him out. Thank God it's no worse. He'll come round."

Not dead? Peter took a long deep breath. He began to explain again. "I saw him stealing Silver Boy."

Mr. Dan looked up. "You shot my guide, my friend, Tallcorn," he said sadly. "He was walking my horse, taking care of him, while I went up the hill a bit."

Mr. Dan's friend, an Indian? Peter could think of nothing to say. He watched while Mr. Dan pushed back the Indian's gray-streaked hair from the wound. It seemed a long time before the Indian grunted, stirred, and raised a hand to his head.

In a guttural voice he said something Peter could not understand.

Mr. Dan answered gravely, "Boy . . . hunting."

The Indian sat up and turned his head to look at Peter. His deep-set eyes seemed to gleam with dark fierceness. Peter looked away, his throat growing tight. "What will he do?" he asked himself. "He knows I shot him, and my gun is empty." He started to reload it.

As the Indian got slowly to his feet, Mr. Dan asked, "Shall we go now? Can you ride Silver Boy?"

Peter glanced up quickly. Did the circuit rider mean to go on without stopping? They had all been waiting for him to come. "You'll stop at the cabin, won't you?" he asked.

"I have a friend with me," Mr. Dan said quietly. His eyes searched Peter's asking plainly, "Will my Indian friend be welcome, too?"

Peter swallowed hard and nodded. Then, remembering, he said, "I shot a possum. Left it back a ways."

"Go after it," Mr. Dan told him. "You can catch up with us. We'll walk slowly."

CHAPTER 12

Good Salt

HEART troubled, thoughts in a tangle, Peter got the possum and trailed after the circuit rider and the Indian. Thinking how the Indian had slumped to the ground, he shivered. "Mighty near killed him," he said aloud. "That's what I was aiming to do."

He thought of what Mr. Dan had asked, in the barn that night. "If you kill an Indian, will that make your folks live again?"

"No," murmured Peter. "Reckon he's got it right. Killing's no good way, just makes you feel worse."

Mr. Dan had added, "There are good Indians, I know."

Peter nodded, remembering the Indian who had saved David from the wildcat. He had meant to tell Mr. Dan about that. Instead, he had wounded Mr. Dan's friend.

Now Mr. Dan and the Indian were on their way to the cabin! What would Uncle Jim and Aunt Libby say? They'd be right glad to see Mr. Dan, but what about his friend? Uncle Jim wanted to live peaceably with redskins, but Aunt Libby would be afraid, and so would Mary Ann.

Peter's feet felt as heavy as his heart. He followed behind Mr. Dan and the Indian. Mr. Dan was talking, the Indian listening, now and again nodding his head. At the clearing Peter caught up with them. He stole a look at the Indian on the horse. His head was still bleeding.

Nip had heard them coming and was barking excitedly. David had spied them. He came running toward them, shouting, "Here's Mr. Dan!" Mary Ann followed David, but stopped short when she saw the Indian on the horse.

Wiping her hands on her apron, Aunt Libby called out as she came from the cabin, "We've been watching out for you." When she saw the Indian, she stepped near to Mary Ann and slipped her arm about Mary Ann's waist.

Uncle Jim came along. "Glad to see you," he said heartily, shaking Mr. Dan's hand. He glanced from Mr. Dan to the Indian and back to Mr. Dan.

"This is my guide and friend, Tallcorn," said the circuit rider with a warm smile for them all. "Peter found us."

"Look, Mammy!" cried David. "The Indian's bleeding on his head."

"Gun wound?" asked Aunt Libby. Tallcorn nodded.

"I'm glad to say it isn't serious," said Mr. Dan.

Peter handed his gun to Uncle Jim and the possum to Mary Ann. He held Silver Boy's bridle while the Indian got down.

"Come," said Aunt Libby, leading the way to the cabin. "We'll take care of that wound."

Peter led Silver Boy into the barn, fed, watered, and rubbed him down. Then, pausing just inside the barn door, he listened to the voices at the cabin —Mr. Dan speaking, then Uncle Jim, and David calling Nip. The redskin was there, too. Peter wished he could forget how the Indian had looked, lying still on the ground, his head bleeding.

"Guess I'd best clean the barn," he told himself.

Any job would do. He didn't want to go where the Indian was.

He was sweeping, raising a dust, when Mary Ann came with a bundle of skins. "Uncle Jim said to get down some stalks for beds. You can use these skins for covers," she said.

"Beds?" questioned Peter. "For the redskin, too?"

"Reckon so," answered Mary Ann. "He's been right alongside the circuit rider these past weeks. Mr. Dan's been trying to preach to some Indians. Tallcorn's been putting the words into Indian talk." She turned away, adding, "Supper's ready."

Peter watched while Mary Ann returned to the cabin. Then, slowly, he dropped the broom and followed her. Outside of the cabin he stopped to wash.

"We're waiting on you, Peter," Aunt Libby called out. Just inside the door, head bandaged, sat the Indian with a bowl of food in his hand.

The misery inside of Peter grew worse as he passed Tallcorn and slid into the vacant place next to Mr. Dan. Uncle Jim filled his bowl with food. Peter took a bite, but he couldn't swallow. Bit by bit, when he thought no one was looking, he fed his supper to Nip.

While they were eating, Aunt Libby said, "Mary Ann and Peter are learning to read, and he's been working hard with the fiddle to surprise you."

Peter gulped. Why did Aunt Libby have to say that? How could he play for Mr. Dan, play his song, after what he'd done?

"I'm looking forward to that," said Mr. Dan. Smiling, he helped himself to another piece of corn bread. "It's good to sit down at a table and enjoy food like this."

David piped up, "It's the salt."

With a wink at Aunt Libby, Uncle Jim added, "It's good for man and beast."

"It is, indeed," agreed Mr. Dan. "And there's another kind of salt that's even better."

"Another kind of salt?" said Aunt Libby, looking puzzled.

"That of friendship and understanding," said Mr. Dan, smiling again. "All of us need it. When we have it everything is good."

The way it was when Uncle Jim came home, thought Peter.

When supper was over, Mr. Dan said, "It's such a beautiful evening, I suggest we sit out under the tree."

Peter carried out a stool, then tried to slip away.

"Where are you going?" asked Aunt Libby.

"To get stalks down for the beds," answered Peter.

"Time enough for that," said Uncle Jim.

Peter came back and sat down. In a quick glance, he saw the Indian sitting on the ground a little way off. He wasn't fierce now. There was gentleness in his dark, lined face. Suddenly he lifted his head and looked toward Peter. Quickly Peter turned away.

Mr. Dan opened his Bible and began to read. Peter tried to listen, but his own thoughts kept interfering. The heaviness on his chest seemed more than he could bear. Then Aunt Libby placed the fiddle in his hands, and he looked up startled.

She said, "Play for Mr. Dan."

With a shake of his head, Peter tried to hand the fiddle back to her.

"What's troubling you, Peter?" Uncle Jim asked quietly.

Peter felt too miserable to speak. Reckon I'll just have to tell them, he thought, and blurted out, "I . . . I did it. I shot Tallcorn. I thought he was taking Mr. Dan's horse."

"Peter!" Aunt Libby cried softly.

For a long moment no one spoke. Then Mr. Dan

said, "We know why it happened, Peter. I have talked with Tallcorn. He understands."

"I'm mighty sorry about this," Uncle Jim was saying.

"Will you play for us now, Peter?" asked Mr. Dan.

Peter looked at the fiddle in his hand. Perhaps it could say what was in his heart. He got up and set it under his chin. Eyes closed, he played, haltingly, his fingers trembling as he felt for the right notes. When the song ended, he passed the fiddle to Aunt Libby, sat down, and bowed his head.

Mr. Dan cleared his throat. "Thank you, Peter," he said in a low voice. He stood up and said quietly, "Shall we pray?"

"Our heavenly Father," he began.

Peter heard a sound and glanced up. The old Indian was standing, too, his face lifted toward the evening sky, his lips moving, as if he were praying. With wonder in his heart, Peter bowed his head again and closed his eyes.

When the prayer ended, he hurried to the barn to get the beds ready. He was bunching some stalks together when someone stood in the doorway, shutting out the light.

Before he turned, Peter knew who it was. A

tightness gathered inside of him as the Indian stepped toward him. When Tallcorn was near, he raised his arm and placed his strong hand firmly on Peter's shoulder.

A lump in his throat made it hard for Peter to speak. But suddenly the heaviness and tightness inside of him were gone. He wanted to speak, to say something. He looked up, gulped, and whispered, "I'm . . . I'm sorry."

The Indian's dark eyes were friendly and kind. He nodded slowly, and a warm happiness surged through Peter. Tallcorn understood. He was a friend. An Indian could be his friend, his neighbor.